629.25

Donated by The Froyer Family, March 2014

Fast Rides

Jet-Powered Speed

by Michael Sandler

Consultant: Mike McNessor
Automotive Journalist

BEARPORT
PUBLISHING

New York, New York

Credits

Cover and Title Page, © Courtesy of Thrust SSC; 4–5, Courtesy of Thrust SSC; 6–7, © British Motor Industry Heritage Trust; 8, © Transtock/SuperStock; 9L, © Transtock/SuperStock; 10, Courtesy of Motor Snaps.com; 11, © Bettmann/Corbis; 12–13, © National Motor Museum/Photolibrary; 14, © U.S. Navy photo by Mass Communication Specialist 2nd Class Lynn Friant; 14–15, © Richard Seaman; 16, © John Chapple/Getty Images; 16–17, © Cody Images/Photo Researchers, Inc.; 18, © AP Images/The Herald/Jennifer Buchanan; 18–19, Courtesy of Landspeed.com/Image by Rachel Shadle; 20, © Courtesy of Bloodhound SSC; 21, © Curventa/Splash News/Newscom.

Publisher: Kenn Goin
Senior Editor: Lisa Wiseman
Creative Director: Spencer Brinker
Design: Debrah Kaiser
Photo Researcher: Picture Perfect Professionals, LLC

Library of Congress Cataloging-in-Publication Data

Sandler, Michael, 1965–
  Jet-powered speed / by Michael Sandler.
    p. cm. — (Fast rides)
  Includes bibliographical references and index.
  ISBN-13: 978-1-61772-136-6 (library binding)
  ISBN-10: 1-61772-136-0 (library binding)
  1. Automobiles, Gas-turbine—Juvenile literature. I. Title.
  TL226.S26 2011
  629.25'05—dc22
                              2010037210

Copyright © 2011 Bearport Publishing Company, Inc. All rights reserved. No part of this publication may be reproduced in whole or in part, stored in a retrieval system, or transmitted in any form or by any means, electronic, mechanical, photocopying, recording, or otherwise, without written permission from the publisher.

For more information, write to Bearport Publishing Company, Inc., 101 Fifth Avenue, Suite 6R, New York, New York 10003. Printed in the United States of America in North Mankato, Minnesota.

113010
10810CGA

10 9 8 7 6 5 4 3 2 1

Table of Contents

Jet-Powered Speed 4
Rover Jet 1 6
Chrysler's Turbine Car 8
Spirit of America 10
Thrust2 12
Shockwave 14
ThrustSSC 16
North American Eagle 18
Bloodhound SSC 20

How a Jet Engine Works 22
Glossary 23
Bibliography 24
Read More 24
Learn More Online 24
Index 24
About the Author 24

Jet-Powered Speed

During the 1800s, the first automobiles barely went ten miles per hour (16 kph)—not much faster than the average person can run! Since then, cars have become much more powerful, and drivers have pushed them to greater and greater speeds. By the 1960s, cars were breaking speed records of more than 600 miles per hour (966 kph). Today, one car, the ThrustSCC, has even **exceeded** the **speed of sound**, which is about 761 miles per hour (1,225 kph).

In 1997, the jet-powered ThrustSSC hit a top speed of 763 miles per hour (1,228 kph).

These high speeds make some automobiles faster than passenger airplanes, which usually go between 500 and 600 miles per hour (805 and 966 kph). What can power a car to zoom so fast? The engine is the key. Not surprisingly, superfast cars don't use ordinary automobile engines. Instead, they use the same engines big airplanes use—**jet engines**.

In this book you will read about the fastest cars in the world. So fasten your seat belt and get ready for jet-powered speed!

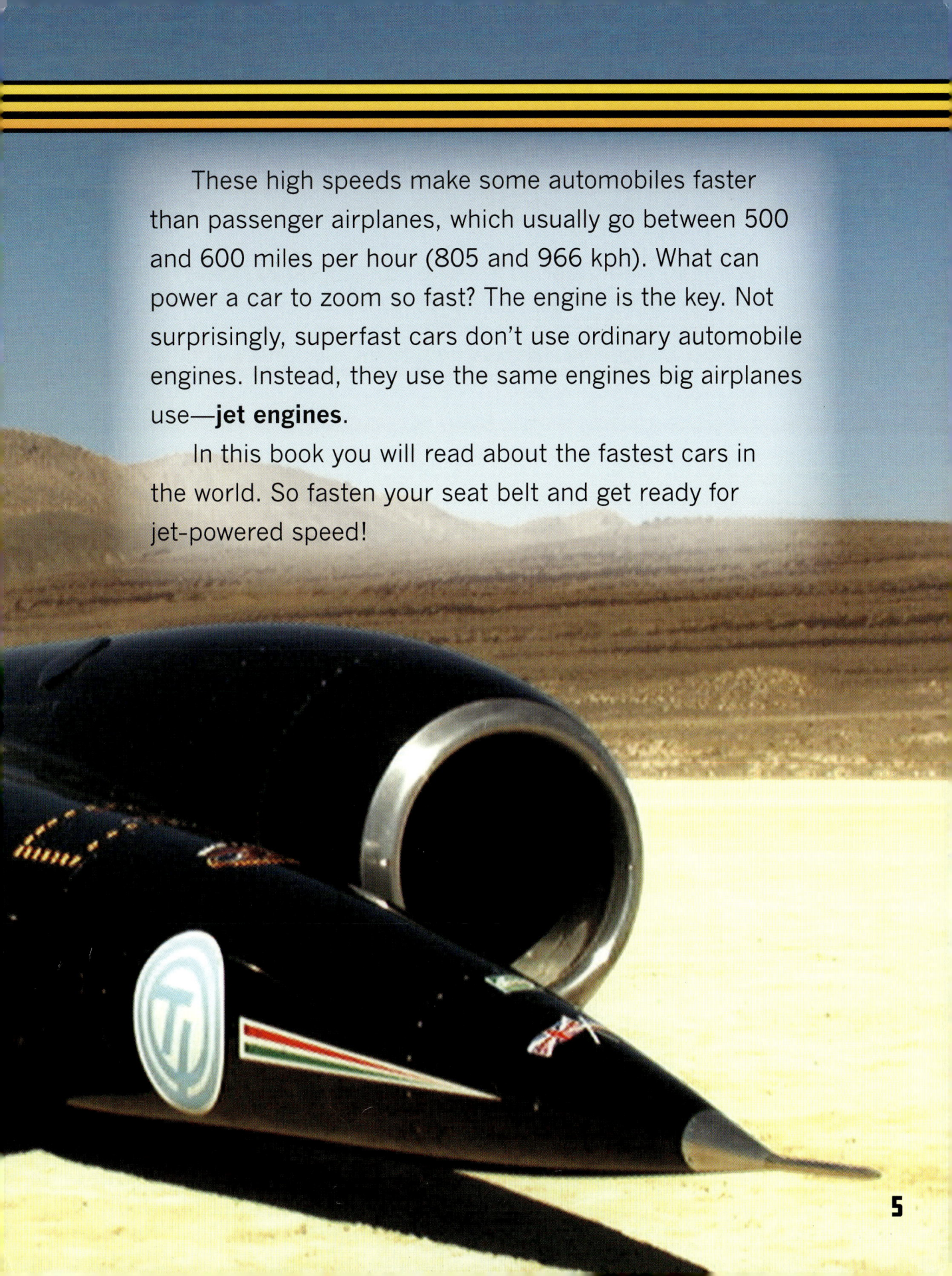

Rover Jet 1

TOP SPEED: 152 miles per hour (245 kph)   **HORSEPOWER:** 200
JET ENGINES: 1   **BUILDER:** Rover

Jet engines first took to the skies on August 27, 1939. On that day, the first jet-powered plane, the Heinkel He-178, roared down a German runway and soared into the air. The Heinkel could fly about 400 miles per hour (644 kph). Later on, jets became even faster. When automobile builders heard about this powerful new type of engine, they wondered if it could be used in cars, too.

Within a few years, automakers were experimenting with putting jet engines in cars. The British car company Rover had worked on producing jet engines for planes during World War II (1939–1945). Then in 1950 they became the first company to produce a jet-powered car called the Rover Jet 1. The sleek two-seater had no roof, but it had plenty of speed for its time. The car ran smoothly and was simple to drive. Unlike other cars that had three pedals, this one had just two—a brake and an **accelerator**. The Jet 1 was purely a test car and was never sold to the public.

The original Rover Jet 1 had a 100-**horsepower** engine and could reach 90 miles per hour (145 kph). With a few **modifications** to the engine, the car got even faster. In 1952, it was clocked moving at more than 150 miles per hour (241 kph) on a test run in Belgium.

The Jet 1 out on the road in the mid-1950s

Chrysler's Turbine Car

TOP SPEED: 115 miles per hour (185 kph) **HORSEPOWER:** 130
JET ENGINES: 1 **BUILDER:** Chrysler

Soon American automakers also started building cars with jet engines. One of these companies, Chrysler, wondered if people would like driving jet-powered cars on an everyday basis. To find out, this Michigan-based manufacturer produced 55 Turbine Cars in 1963. The company loaned out 50 of these cars for three-month-long test drives.

Drivers loved the futuristic Turbines, which looked a lot like a fighter jet from the back. The cars, which could seat a family of four, were **luxurious**. They had leather seats and power windows. The look of the Turbine attracted attention wherever it was driven, causing people to stop and stare.

From the back, the Chrysler Turbine looked a lot like a fighter jet.

More than 30,000 people applied to test-drive the Turbine. Over a two year period, only 203 lucky people got the chance. Those who did drove the cars as much as possible, knowing they had to return their Turbine after 90 days.

Chrysler hoped to sell future versions of the Turbine but never did. Jet engines were powerful, but they proved to be too expensive. Only nine of the cars still exist. Chrysler destroyed the rest after testing was completed.

The Chrysler Turbine

Spirit of America

TOP SPEED: 601 miles per hour (967 kph) **HORSEPOWER:** 15,000
JET ENGINES: 1   **BUILDER:** Craig Breedlove

While jet engines may not be good for everyday cars, they are perfect for setting speed records. Car builder and racer Craig Breedlove proved this with his Spirit of America.

The 1963 Spirit of America

In different models of this jet-powered car, Breedlove broke the world land-speed record five different times between 1963 and 1965. His first Spirit was long and **rocket**-shaped with a single fin in the back. Since it had only three wheels, some called it a tricycle and said it wasn't really a car. Whatever it was, the Spirit made Breedlove the fastest driver on the planet when it blasted across the Utah desert at 407 miles per hour (655 kph) on October 5, 1963.

His second model of the car, the Spirit of America Sonic 1, had four wheels and was even more powerful than the first. It reached a top speed of 601 miles per hour (967 kph) on November 15, 1965.

Craig Breedlove was the first driver to go faster than 400 miles per hour (644 kph). He was also the first to go faster than 500, and later 600 miles per hour (805, 966 kph). He set all these records in different Spirit of America models on the **Bonneville Salt Flats** in Utah.

The Spirit of America Sonic 1

Thrust2

TOP SPEED: 633 miles per hour (1,019 kph)   **HORSEPOWER:** 35,000
JET ENGINES: 1   **BUILDER:** Richard Noble

Englishman Richard Noble had a dream. He wanted to break the land-speed record in a British automobile. To do so, he built a sleek and **swoopy** supercar called the Thrust2. This 27-foot (8 m) long car was made of strong steel and lightweight aluminum. At the heart of the car was a huge **Rolls-Royce** jet engine that came from a British fighter jet.

On October 4, 1983, the Thrust2 roared across Nevada's **Black Rock Desert** at 633 miles per hour (1,019 kph), leaving behind a dust trail 30 feet (9 m) high and 10 miles (16 km) long. At the time, Noble's jet-powered speedster was the fastest car in the world.

The Thrust2 didn't just use brakes to stop. Three parachutes popped out of the back of the car to help it slow down.

The Thrust2

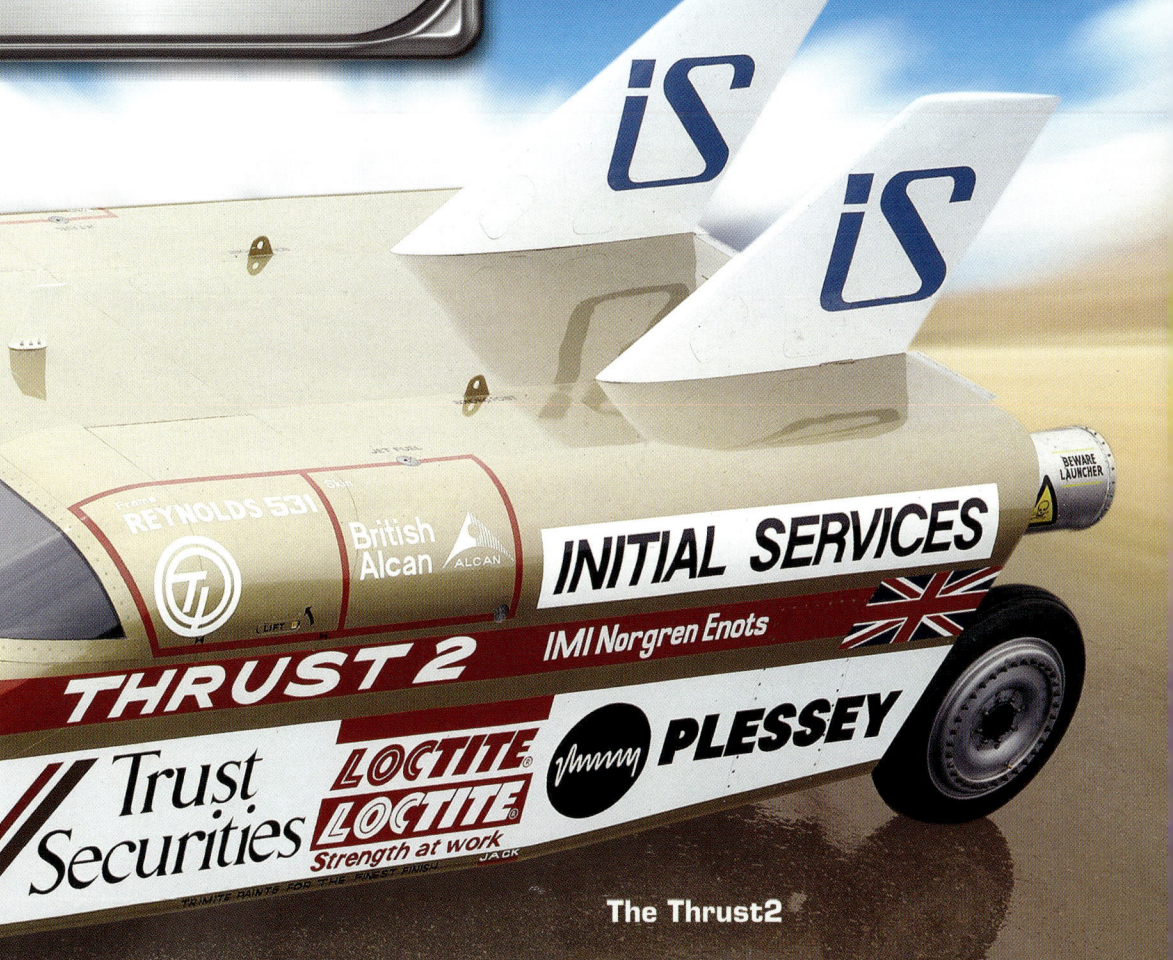

Shockwave

TOP SPEED: 376 miles per hour (605 kph)   **HORSEPOWER:** 36,000
JET ENGINES: 3   **BUILDER:** Les Shockley

Cars aren't the only jet-**propelled** land vehicles. People have used jet engines in trucks as well. Shockwave, the world's fastest truck, is a 7,000-pound (3,175-kg) monster powered by not one but three jet engines.

When the big truck revs up its engines, huge flames from the back shoot into the air. It takes a lot of fuel to get those engines moving. Shockwave uses 120 gallons (454 l) of diesel fuel in a quarter-mile (.4-km) run! An average car could travel 3,000 miles (4,828 km) on the same amount of fuel.

Naturally, a truck like this isn't used to haul things around. Shockwave is a show truck that appears at air and car shows as well as **drag races**. During these shows, Shockwave often races against planes—and usually comes out the winner!

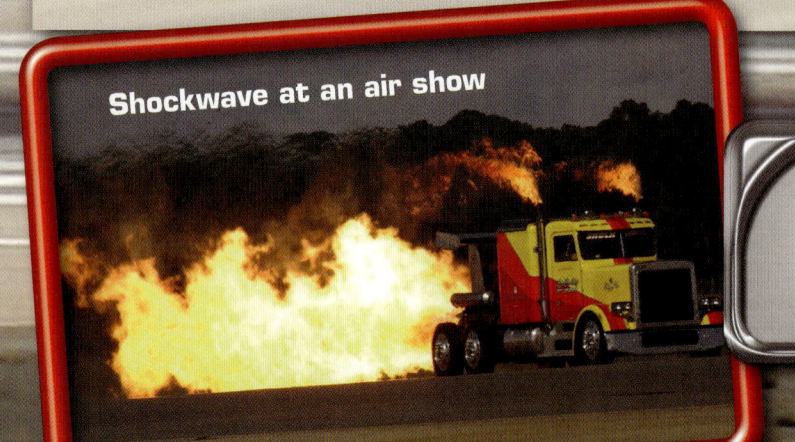

Shockwave at an air show

Shockwave holds the speed record for trucks—376 miles per hour (605 kph).

Shockwave races against a fighter jet.

15

ThrustSSC

TOP SPEED: 763 miles per hour (1,228 kph)   **HORSEPOWER:** 110,000
JET ENGINES: 2   **BUILDER:** Richard Noble

In 1947, U.S. Air Force pilot Chuck Yeager became the first person to travel faster than the speed of sound. He did it while he was flying the Bell X-1, a rocket-powered plane. Fifty years later, in 1997, Andy Green traveled faster than the speed of sound on land. How? He used a jet-powered car.

Andy Green and the ThrustSCC

Green, a British Air Force pilot, was driving the ThrustSSC, the British follow-up to the Thrust2. The car, which was 54 feet (16 m) long and weighed 10 tons (9 metric tons), had twin jet engines, one mounted on each side of the driver's **cockpit**. It roared across the Black Rock Desert, creating a massive **sonic boom** when it went faster than the speed of sound. Miles and miles away, buildings shook from the noise.

In 1997, Andy Green set two records in the ThrustSSC. On September 25, he became the first person to drive more than 700 miles per hour (1,127 kph), actually reaching 714 miles per hour (1,149 kph). Then about three weeks later, he went faster than the speed of sound when he drove the ThrustSSC to 763 miles per hour (1,228 kph).

Andy Green reaching 714 miles per hour (1,149 kph) in the ThrustSCC

North American Eagle

PROJECTED SPEED: 800 miles per hour (1,288 kph) **HORSEPOWER:** 52,000
JET ENGINES: 1 **BUILDER:** North American Eagle Team

ThrustSSC's speed record has lasted for more than a decade. However, it may not hold up much longer. A group of 40 American and Canadian volunteers are working hard to bring the land-speed record back to North America.

Volunteers working on the North American Eagle

The car they are building, the North American Eagle, is half high-tech and half junkyard scrap. The long, slender speedster has parts from an old Lockheed F-104 Starfighter attack jet as well as custom-made aluminum wheels. Why no rubber tires? At **supersonic** speeds, the rubber would turn to jelly!

The Eagle is being tested at Black Rock Desert, and has already ripped across the sand at more than 400 miles per hour (644 kph). If team leaders Ed Shadle and Keith Zanghi succeed, it will soon be cruising at double that speed.

The North American Eagle at Black Rock Desert

In the late 1950s, the F-104 Starfighter was the world's fastest plane, clocking in at 1,404 miles per hour (2,260 kph). Its engine is now what powers the North American Eagle.

Bloodhound SSC

PROJECTED SPEED: 1,000–1,050 miles per hour (1,609–1,690 kph)
HORSEPOWER: about 130,000   **JET ENGINES:** 1   **BUILDER:** Bloodhound SSC team

Of course, the British would love to hold on to the land-speed record. To keep it, Richard Noble and Andy Green are working on a follow-up to the ThrustSSC. The $17 million car is called the Bloodhound SSC. Its designers have dreams of it reaching 1,000 miles per hour (1,609 kph) or more. To do so, the Bloodhound SSC will use both jet and rocket power.

Richard Noble (left) and Andy Green (right), with a model of the Bloodhound SSC, are leading the car-building team.

A rocket will be bolted on top of a **Eurofighter Typhoon** jet engine. The jet engine will fire up first, taking the 44-foot (13.4-m) long car to about 300 miles per hour (483 kph). Then the rocket will kick in and hopefully bring the Bloodhound to record-breaking speeds. Will it work? The world should know in 2012. That's when the Bloodhound is scheduled to be finished.

rocket

jet engine

A model of the Bloodhound SSC

How fast will the Bloodhound SSC be? With as much power as 250 sports cars, it will travel faster than a speeding bullet. The Bloodhound will be able to cross the distance of four football fields in a single second.

How a Jet Engine Works

A jet engine uses a fan to suck in air. Once inside the engine, the air is compressed—squeezed so it fits inside a small space—and then sprayed with fuel. When this mixture of fuel and air is **ignited**, it **expands** and blasts out the back of the engine. This high-speed stream of air forces a plane—or a car—forward.

1. Fan
The big spinning fan sucks in large amounts of air.

2. Compressor
After going through the fan, the air flows into the compressor. Here, it's squeezed to fit inside a small area.

3. Combuster
The compressor then forces the squeezed air into the combuster. Here, it's mixed with fuel and is ignited, creating very hot, high-**energy** air.

Air Flow

Air Flow

4. Turbine
The very hot, high-energy air blows out of the combuster into the turbine. The fiery air has so much energy that it causes the turbine's blades to spin. This spinning powers the fan, bringing more air into the engine.

5. Nozzle
Finally, the super-heated air from the turbine passes through the nozzle, its last stop in the engine. As the air shoots out of the nozzle, it creates the thrust that causes the plane or car to move forward.

GLOSSARY

accelerator (ak-SEL-uh-*rate*-ur) the pedal in a car that is used to control its speed

Black Rock Desert (BLAK ROK DEH-zurt) a desert area in northern Nevada often used for testing fast cars and setting speed records

Bonneville Salt Flats (BONN-uh-vil SAWLT FLATS) a hard, flat salt plain in the Utah desert often used for testing fast cars and setting speed records

cockpit (KOK-pit) the place where a driver sits in a race car or airplane

drag races (DRAG RAYSS-iz) races in which two vehicles achieve very high speeds over a short, straight track

energy (EN-ur-jee) the power that machines such as cars and planes need in order to work

Eurofighter Typhoon (YOO-roh-fite-ur tye-FOON) a type of jet plane used by the air forces of many European countries

exceeded (ek-SEED-id) gone beyond, passed

expands (ek-SPANDZ) grows bigger

horsepower (HORSS-*pou*-ur) one measure of an engine's power; a single unit of horsepower provides enough energy to power five very bright lightbulbs

ignited (ig-NITE-id) heated up or caused fuel to burn

jet engines (JET EN-juhnz) engines, usually used in airplanes, that shoot out streams of hot gases that push vehicles forward

luxurious (lug-ZHUR-ee-uhss) very comfortable and of high quality

modifications (MOD-uh-fuh-*kay*-shuhnz) changes; improvements

propelled (pruh-PELD) moved or pushed forward

rocket (ROK-it) a vehicle or device shaped like a long tube that has a powerful engine which shoots out hot gases; also used for space travel

Rolls-Royce (ROHLZ-ROYSS) one of the world's most important makers of aircraft engines

sonic boom (SON-ik BOOM) the loud noise that is heard when a car or plane goes faster than the speed of sound

speed of sound (SPEED UHV SOUND) the rate at which a sound wave travels through the air—about 761 miles per hour (1,225 kph)

supersonic (*soo*-pur-SON-ik) faster than the speed of sound

swoopy (SWOOP-ee) having sweeping lines or movements

Bibliography

Cohen, David. "The 1000 mph Car." *New Scientist* (November 18, 2009).

Oerzen, Bobby. "Need for Speed." *Current Science* (February 26, 2009).

Spinelli, Mike. "The Race to 1,000 MPH." *Popular Science* (October 2009).

Todd Lassa. "Road Test: 1964 Chrysler Turbine Car." *Motor Trend* (March 2006).

autospeed.com/cms/title_The-Chrysler-Turbine-Car/A_108220/article.html

news.bbc.co.uk/onthisday/hi/dates/stories/march/8/newsid_2516000/2516271.stm

Read More

Dubowski, Mark. *Superfast Cars.* New York: Bearport (2006).

Graham, Ian. *Fast Cars (How Machines Work).* Ontario, Canada: Saunders (2009).

Graham, Ian. *Supercars (Fast!).* London: QED (2010).

Learn More Online

To learn more about jet-powered cars, visit
www.bearportpublishing.com/FastRides

Index

Black Rock Desert 13, 17, 19
Bloodhound SSC 20–21
Bonneville Salt Flats 11
Breedlove, Craig 10–11
Chrysler's Turbine Car 8–9
Green, Andy 16–17, 20
Noble, Richard 12–13, 16, 20
North American Eagle 18–19
Rover Jet 1 6–7
Shadle, Ed 19
Shockley, Les 14
Shockwave 14–15
speed of sound 4, 16–17
Spirit of America 10–11
ThrustSSC 4–5, 16–17, 18, 20
Thrust2 12–13
Yeager, Chuck 16
Zanghi, Keith 19

About the Author

Brooklyn-based writer Michael Sandler has written numerous books on sports, from drag racing to football, for kids and teens.